This book
belongs to:

- - - - - - - - - - - - - - - - -

For Jenny Hayes, with thanks and love,
K.S.

Sir Charlie Stinky Socks would like to donate 10% of the royalties
from the sale of this book to Naomi House Children's Hospice.

EGMONT
brings stories to life

First published in Great Britain in 2016
by Egmont UK Limited
The Yellow Building, 1 Nicholas Road, London W11 4AN
www.egmont.co.uk

Text and illustrations copyright © Kristina Stephenson 2016

Kristina Stephenson has asserted her moral rights.

ISBN (HB) 978 14052 68134
ISBN (PB) 978 14052 68141

A CIP catalogue record for this book is available from the British Library.

Stay safe online. Egmont is not responsible for content hosted by third parties.

THE MUMMY'S GOLD

Kristina Stephenson

EGMONT

Once up☉n the
drifting dunes
of a **desert** in a far-away land,

three figures were dutifully trudging
over the shifting sand.

A **_burly baker_**,
who used to be a **pirate**,
had sent them on a quest:

to return a bag, stolen from
someone in a **desert**
across the sea.

"I've given back the rest of our booty.
Now all that's left is this," he said.
"It's **bashed** and **battered**
and **terribly tattered**,
but it might be precious to that *someone*.

The thing is . . .

I'm too busy baking
to return it."

And that's how it came to be that . . .

...Sir Charlie Stinky Socks, his faithful cat Envelope and, of course, his good grey mare, were there, in the **desert** with a bag and some buns on the brink of a brilliant adventure.

For inside the bag was:

a stick,

some string,

a stone that looked like a *toe*, and . . .

a little leather journal.

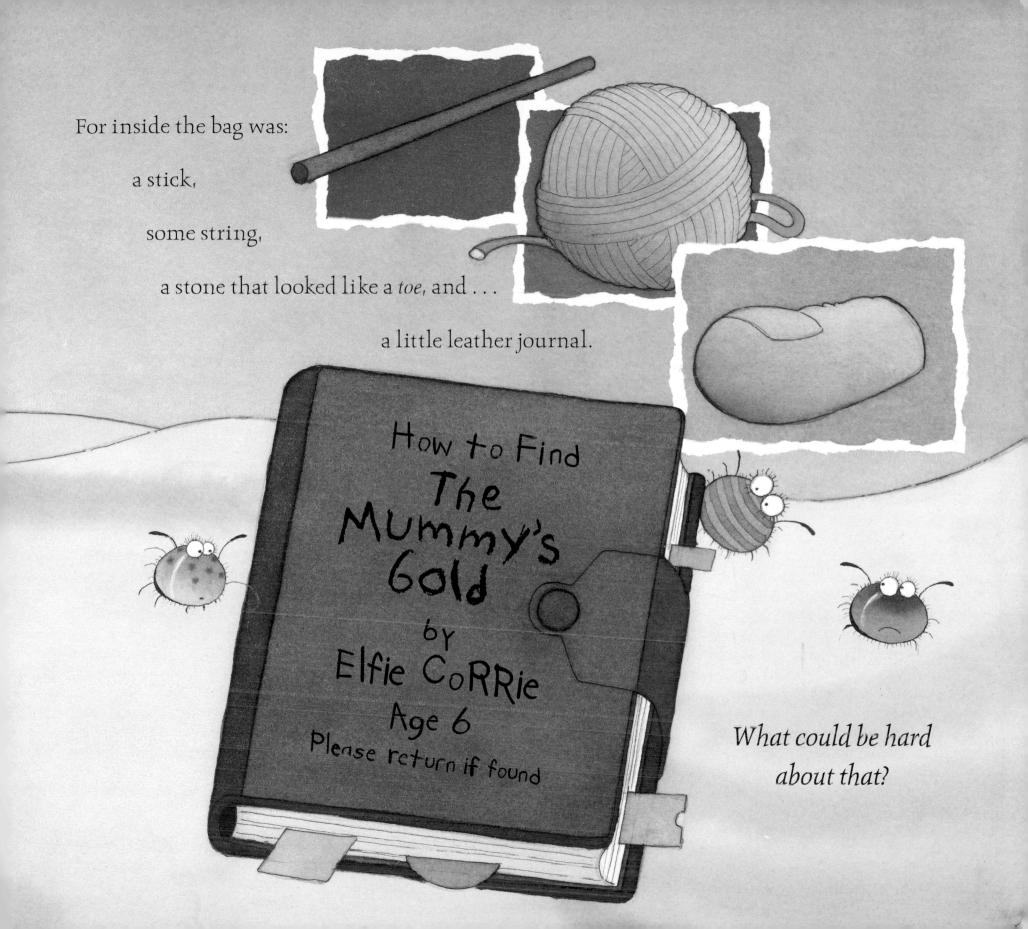

How to Find
The
Mummy's
Gold
by
Elfie CoRRie
Age 6
Please return if found

*What could be hard
about that?*

But, gosh! It was hot!

And not a good place to discover
your bottle's been leaking.

Yikes!

Poor parched cat and overheated horse!

What *were* they going to do?

Just then a **caravan of curious camels** came cruising into view.

"Salutations!" said Sir Charlie
to the *fellow* at the front.
Might we trouble you for a drink?
I don't think my friends and I will make it,
if we haven't any water."

"Make it to where?" asked the *friendly fellow*.

"We're looking for someone," Sir Charlie replied.
"Someone called **Elfie Corrie**.
I believe this bag belongs to her,
because it says so on this book.

Look!"

The *friendly fellow's* eyes lit up.

"**Elfie Corrie**!" he said.
"*I* know where she lives.
And there's a watering hole
on the way.

Why don't I take you there?"

The knight and his cat were glad of the ride.

The good grey mare wasn't sure.

But it wasn't long before they came to an oasis.

"Drink your fill," said the *friendly fellow*.

"I will make camp for the night."

He lit a fire, pitched his tent, and told
Sir Charlie and his friends to go in.

"Sleep," he said. "I'll keep watch.
I don't want your bag to be stolen."

ZZZZZZZZZZZZZZZZZ

It was already hot when the friends woke up
to find the **camels** had **gone** –
along with the *friendly fellow*.

Sir Charlie scratched his head.

"Well, at least we still have the bag," he said.
"And this tent will come in handy."

It did!

In the guise of a **camel** the
good grey mare sailed across the **desert**.

Swish, swish, swishity-swish!

Straight to a one horse town and . . .

CORRIE'S CURIOSITIES
MUSEUM OF MARVELLOUS THINGS

OPEN

Noticing the name
was the same as **Elfie's**,
Sir Charlie ventured in . . .

"You see, when I was six," **Elfie** said,
"I planned a **really big adventure**.

I'd heard the stories about the missing **gold**
of the **Pharaoh Aboo Ra** –
lost in the desert for thousands of years.

So I decided to find it!

I wrote down clues in my journal
and collected things to use on the way,
until inside my bag I had **everything** I needed
to find the **mummy's gold**.

Except . . ." she said,

"for one last thing and
while I was searching for it,
someone stole my bag."

Oh my!

"When I grew up," Elfie continued, "I became an explorer.
I found all kinds of trinkets and treasures,
but I didn't find my bag.
So I never had my **really big adventure** and now . . .
I'm just too old.

"That's silly!" said Sir Charlie kindly.
**"You're never too old
for adventure**.
And I'd be happy to help you."

Elfie thought for a moment or two.

Then she smiled at the little knight.

"By golly, you're right," she said
to Sir Charlie. "**Let's go and
find that gold.**"

She opened her bag
to take out her journal, but . . .

"I saw those feet on the way," said Sir Charlie. "And my . . . erm . . . camel can take us there."

Clue number 1:
Two giant feet
stand alone in the sand."

"Not to worry," said Elfie. "He's got the journal, but he won't find the **gold** without the other things in this bag. I might be old," she said with a smile, "but I've still got the clues in my head."

. . . where *was* the little book?

Oh no!

"That *not-so-friendly fellow* I met
must have taken it," said Sir Charlie.
"I'll bet he's after the **gold**!"

Trudge, trudge, trudge, trudge!

Over the shifting sand, to the remains
of a statue with only nine toes.

"Clue number 2!" said Elfie.

"When the last toe lies
in its rightful place,
behold the secret door."

Elfie took out her toe-shaped stone.

But that's when
Sir Charlie saw the *not-so-friendly fellow*!
He'd got to the feet first.

Drat!

Time for a mare with a bag of buns to tempt the **camels** away.
Off they trotted after the buns, followed by the
not-so-friendly fellow who wanted his **camels** back.

Elfie popped the toe
in its place and . . .

Behold! The secret door.

Down a flight of steep stone steps went the intrepid explorers.

"We'd better hurry!" said Sir Charlie, "before that *fellow* comes back."

Pitter-patter.
Pitter-patter.

Past a petrified cat —

yikes.

Not daring to look at the grisly guardians of the **Pharaoh Aboo Ra**

Trip trap, trip trap, to . . . .

a mighty mystical maze where people could get lost for days.

Then . . . .

Elfie remembered the next clue.

"String will bring you back to safety,
should the path you take be untrue."

"Got it!" said the clever knight, fastening one
end of Elfie's string to a figure on the wall.

"One wrong turn," he said to the others,
"and we simply follow this back.
Anyway . . . I'm good at mazes."

Maybe you are too?

Start

finish

Beyond the maze was a decorated door.

It was locked.

There was no way in.

"Botheration!" said Sir Charlie.

But **Elfie Corrie** was smiling.

"Look at the picture
on the wall," she said.
"It's just as I thought
it would be.

Glittering **gold** and untold *treasures*
filled the ancient tomb,
and in the middle stood . . .

the **mumbling mummy**
of the
Pharaoh Aboo Ra!

"Thieves!"
he grumbled, "you've come
to steal my **gold**."

Oh what luck!

They were just in time.

Back came the *not-so-friendly fellow*, leading a line of munching **camels**, and a mightily proud, grey mare.

"I'm sorry," he said when he saw Elfie, and he handed her the book. "I only took it because I wanted to have a **really big adventure.**"

"Then we'd better make sure you have one," said Elfie. "Come to my shop tomorrow. I've got **marvellous maps** from around the world; one of them should do."

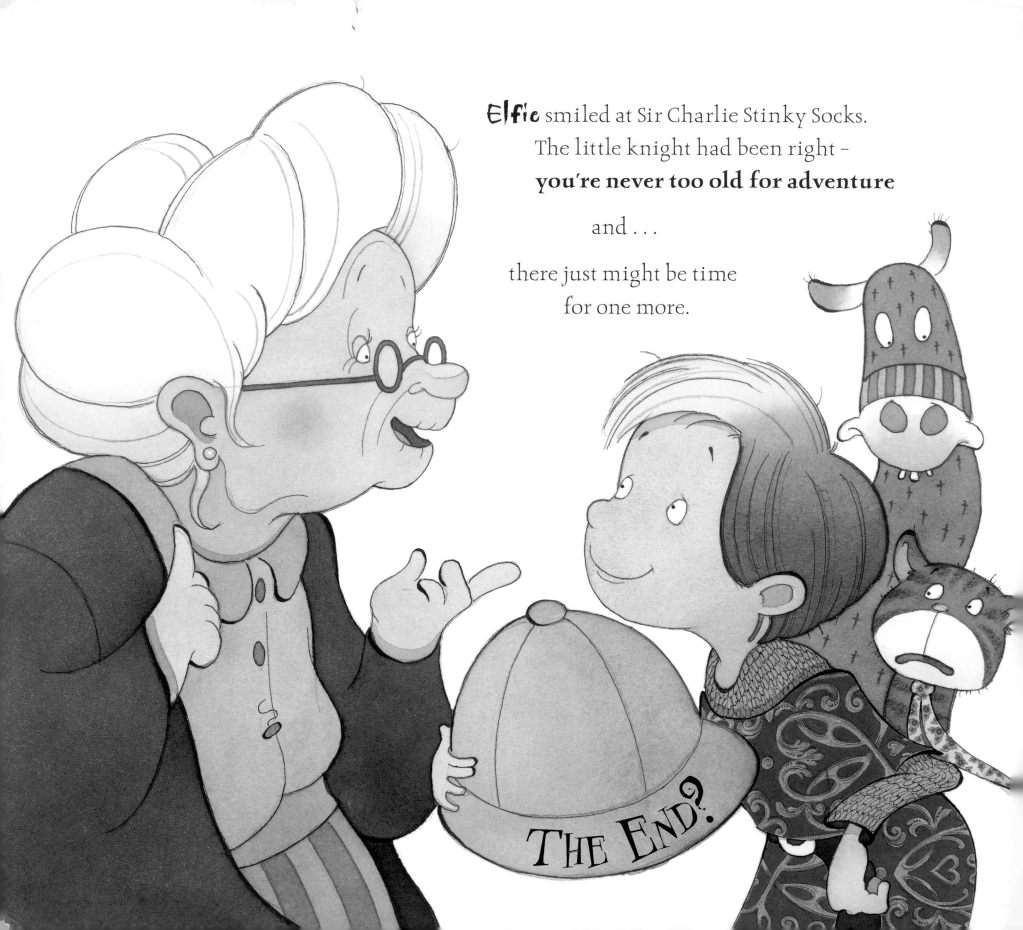

Elfie smiled at Sir Charlie Stinky Socks.
The little knight had been right –
you're never too old for adventure

and . . .

there just might be time
for one more.

THE END?